For Michael with love – C.F

For Harry – M.B

First published 2018 by Macmillan Children's Books
an imprint of Pan Macmillan,
20 New Wharf Road, London N1 9RR
Associated companies throughout the world
www.panmacmillan.com

ISBN: 978-1-5098-3078-7

1 3 5 7 9 8 6 4 2

A CIP catalogue record for this book is available
from the British Library.

Printed in China.

There's a SPIDER in this Book!

Written by
CLAIRE FREEDMAN

Illustrated by
MIKE BYRNE

Can you spot me inside?

Macmillan Children's Books

Hello!

I should probably warn you - there's a spider in this book! My name is Eric. I have long hairy legs and big googly eyes.

Granny and Fluffy the cat don't like spiders, so I'm hiding.
Can you find me?

Stop shouting my name!

I am NOT coming out. You will probably be really scared of me and run away.

Here is a picture of some cute bunnies
for you to look at instead.

I don't care how many times you call out Eric.
And it's no good shaking the book.
I'm NOT coming out.

But, to show you there are no hard feelings,
here is a lovely little present.
I wrapped it up myself.

You don't like it?
Talk about ungrateful!

Perhaps if people got to know the real me,
they wouldn't be so scared of spiders.

My favourite hobby is embroidery,

I can run really fast too.

Especially when Fluffy
is trying to eat me!

It's not easy being me, you know.
People scream at me all the time,
which doesn't do my confidence any good.

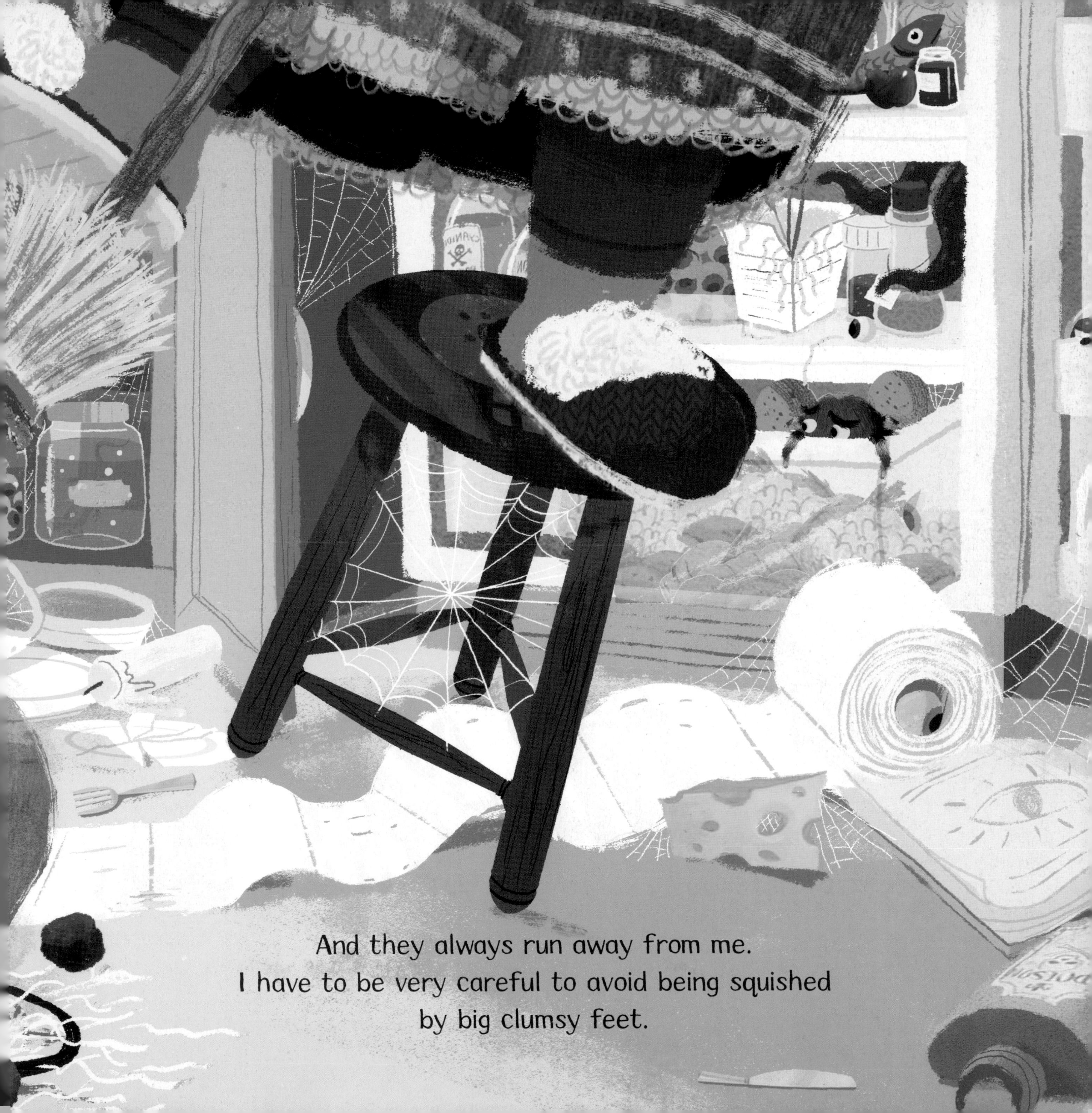

And they always run away from me.
I have to be very careful to avoid being squished
by big clumsy feet.

Think of it from my point of view . . .

People poke me with long, pointy sticks,

they trap me in jam jars then throw me out of high windows . . .

. . . and worst of all is that noisy sucking machine.

It's not fair. Pick on someone your own size! My nerves are in shreds.

I've tried to get people to like me.
One Christmas, to look less frightening
I disguised myself as a decoration on Granny's tree.

BIG
MISTAKE!

If people weren't so scared of me,
I'd make an excellent pet.

I could catch any flies buzzing round their home.

I wouldn't need feeding.

And they'd never need to brush me.

I really like playing games too. I'm great at hide-and-seek.

And Fluffy is never smart
enough to catch me . . .

CRASH!

See what I mean?

Unfortunately, Fluffy doesn't enjoy our games as much as me.

And he hates being told off. It makes him really mad.
Good job I have an emergency escape line. Quick! Turn the page!

Phew! That was close.

Inside this book is a brilliant place to hide.
I bet you still can't find me!